Lily in the *Loft*

written by *Carol L. MacKay*

illustrated by *Val Moker*

REGINA, SASKATCHEWAN

LILY IN THE LOFT
Story © Carol L. MacKay, 2017
Illustrations © Val Moker, 2017
All rights reserved.

Published by Your Nickel's Worth Publishing.
April 2017

Library and Archives Canada Cataloguing in Publication

MacKay, Carol L., author
     Lily in the loft / written by Carol L. MacKay ; illustrated by Val Moker.

ISBN 978-1-927756-91-1 (softcover)

     I. Moker, Val, 1954-, illustrator II. Title.

PS8625.K3882L55 2017   JC813'.6   C2016-907765-9

Printed in Canada.

21 20 19 18 17   1 2 3 4 5

Book design by Heather Nickel.
Production made possible with the support of Creative Saskatchewan.

MIX
Paper from responsible sources
FSC® C016245

YOUR NICKEL'S WORTH PUBLISHING

www.ynwp.ca

For Sister Ann and Bluebird.

— C.M.

For Carol for allowing me this journey;
for my husband, Gord, and son, Alex, for putting up with my work schedule;
for Claire, my model and inspiration;
and lastly, for Chevy (the cat), for posing it up!

— V.M.

Frances loved the loft.
She sat near the hay
door with her
notebook and pencil
and scribbled poems
and stories.

From the hayloft she could see the surrounding fields of wheat and oats,
and off to the west, the cattle grazing in the pasture.

There was so much to write about on the farm.

Frances had already filled up one of the three notebooks
she had gotten from Aunt Margaret for her birthday.

Her aunt had also shown her a farm newspaper where she could send her writing, but Frances wasn't sure she was good enough. Not many people knew she liked to write. Frances didn't speak up much in school and only her best friend Nancy knew that she wrote poems and stories.

Aunt Margaret showed
her that she could use
a pen-name so that
anyone reading the
newspaper wouldn't
know who she was.

There were two pages in the newspaper called "The Young Co-operators' Club" or "YC Club" for short.

THE WESTERN PRODUCER AUGUST 17, 1947

YOUNG CO-OPERATORS

NATURE

FLOWERS FRESH

HERON
(by Phantom Yodeller)

SOME SATURDAY
Prairie Lily
(by Maisie)

BUTTERFLIES
— Gypsy Melody —

Everyone who wrote in was between the ages of eight and twenty-one, and nearly everyone used a pen-name.

Some of the pen-names were intriguing, like "Gypsy Melody," or "Phantom Yodeller." Some were just nice names, like "Maisie."

"What would you pick for a pen-name?"
asked Aunt Margaret.

Frances thought for a few seconds.
"I'd be called Lily in the Loft."

"That's a great name. Why Lily?"
asked Aunt Margaret.

"It's my favourite flower,"
said Frances.

So Frances wrote her favourite poem in her best handwriting on a new sheet of paper and put it in an envelope. She took four pennies from her savings jar and went to the post office. She bought a stamp from the postmaster and mailed away her poem.

Frances knew that if the editor, "Sister Ann" (who also used a pen-name), liked her poem enough to print it, she would become a member of the club.

"But what if
they don't like my poem?"
Frances asked Aunt Margaret.

"I'm sure they will like it, but
they still might not print it.
They can't print every poem
they get, but if you want to
be a writer, you'll just have
to keep writing and send
them something else. That's
how writing works," said
Aunt Margaret.

The next Thursday, Frances had a tough time concentrating at school.

It was newspaper day.

She ran all the way home, down the dusty gravel road to the farm, and burst through the front door.

"Did the paper come?"

"It's on the kitchen table," said her mother.

YOUNG CO-O

PURE LOVE

SKY

BIRDS

Frances flipped through the newspaper pages about grain and cattle prices, the recipes, and the sewing section, until she found The Young Co-operators' pages.

But her poem was not there.

Frances had a chance to read a few of the poems before her mother reminded her that she was supposed to clean out the chicken coop.

As Frances changed into her work clothes, she wondered if Sister Ann had liked her poem at all.

The week went by slowly.

When Frances checked the next issue of the newspaper on the following Thursday, her poem was not in the paper.

It wasn't in the next week's newspaper either, or the one after that.

THE WESTERN P

Frances was certain the editor must not have liked her poem.

After a month of waiting, Frances didn't feel like sharing her poetry anymore. It mustn't be very good, she thought.

She sat by the hay door and just watched the sun go down over the pasture.

Lily in the Loft would never see her writing in print.

Frances decided to stop looking for her poem in the newspaper. She would just write for herself.

Over the next few weeks, Frances filled up another one of Aunt Margaret's notebooks with new poems. When Frances flipped through the notebooks, she liked what she read.

Not bad, Frances thought. *Even if no one else likes my poems, I do.*

The next Thursday, even though it was newspaper day, Frances did not run down the gravel road to home and she didn't burst through the front door. Instead, she walked home and headed straight to her room to change into her chore clothes.

Holding the newspaper in her hand,
Frances's mother stopped her as
Frances climbed the stairs.

"Don't you want to check the paper for your poem?" her mother asked.

"It's not in there," Frances replied. "I'm sure they decided not to print it."

"Oh, that's too bad. By the way, this letter arrived for you in the mail." Frances's mother held out an envelope.

Frances let out a little whoop, and ran back down the stairs. She never got letters.

Sometimes, if Aunt Margaret went visiting somewhere interesting, she'd send Frances a postcard.

But no one ever sent her a real letter.

She tore open the envelope.

It was from the newspaper!

Sister
c/o W[...]
Box
Saska[...]

Dear Frances (Lily in the Loft),

Thank you for sending your delightful poem to the YC pages. We will be publishing it in our next issue.

We are happy you joined our writing club and we hope to read many more poems and stories from you.

Sincerely,
Sister Ann

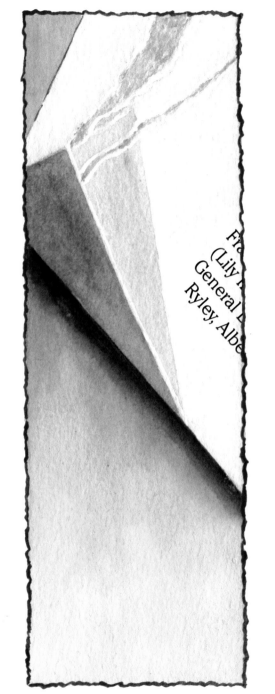

Fra[...]
(Lily [...]
General [...]
Ryley, Albe[...]

The next issue?

Frances looked at her mother, who was still holding the newspaper under her arm.

"Mom, can I see that paper, please?" asked Frances.

"Certainly," said her mother.

Frances rushed to the kitchen table and began to flip through the paper, looking for the YC pages.

"Page 48," said her mother.

"You knew?" said Frances as she turned to page 48.

"Well, I know you are Lily in the Loft, so that poem on page 48 must be yours," her mother said.

PAGE 48

And there it was!

Frances knew that it wouldn't be her last.

YOUNG CO

NATURE

My Favourite Spot

Here in the loft, all is quiet,
just the faint rustle of straw
beneath kitten feet as
Little Calico stretches like a
plant towards the sun.
Her fur is as shiny as a lake
in August,
warm as a pebble on the beach in July.

Here in the loft, all is quiet,
except for the sound of my pen as it
scribbles towards the end of each line.
My words, as blue as the duck pond
to the west,
fly across a pale paper sky.

— *Lily in the Loft*

NATURE

My Favourite Spot

Here in the loft, all is quiet,
just the faint rustle of straw
beneath kitten feet as
Little Calico stretches like a
plant towards the sun.
Her fur is as shiny as a lake
in August,
warm as a pebble on the beach in July.

Here in the loft, all is quiet,
except for the sound of my pen as it
scribbles towards the end of each line.
My words, as blue as the duck pond
to the west,
fly across a pale paper sky.

— *Lily in the Loft*

About the Young Co-operators' Club

The Young Co-operators' Club began in January 1927 when Violet McNaughton, the women's editor of the *Western Producer* in Saskatoon, Saskatchewan, felt that young people across Canada should have their very own place to see their poems and stories in print. Young writers from across Canada, but especially the Prairies, began to send in riddles, poems and stories to "The Pages." The club further developed with the election of leaders and poet laureates from the membership, who would judge the writing that appeared in the YC pages.

Some of the children who wrote in became professional poets, novelists, editors, publishers, screenwriters, bloggers and sports writers when they grew up.

The Young Co-operators' Club published its last page on November 24, 1994. For 67 years it encouraged young Canadian writers to express their ideas, concerns, and creativity in print.

About the Author

Carol L. MacKay grew up in Ryley, Alberta, where she spent many hours crafting poems and stories to send to the Young Co-operators' Pages. Her first poem was published in 1975 under her YC pen-name, "Peppermint Patty." Today, she writes books for young readers, as well as poems and stories for children's magazines like *Highlights, Cricket, Ladybug,* and *Babybug*. She lives on Vancouver Island, British Columbia.

About the Illustrator

Award-winning artist Val Moker has degrees in education and fine art from the University of Saskatchewan. In addition to her work as a professional artist, she has taught art in the education system, and has created art and culture lesson plans for Learning Through the Arts, a structured curriculum development program of the Royal Conservatory of Music in Toronto. Her work has been included in numerous art collections. Val lives with her family in Regina, Saskatchewan. www.valmoker.com